COTTAGE
WOODS
in the

JESSICA CROSS

WESTBOW
PRESS®
A DIVISION OF THOMAS NELSON
& ZONDERVAN

WestBow Press books may be ordered through booksellers or by contacting:

WestBow Press
A Division of Thomas Nelson & Zondervan
1663 Liberty Drive
Bloomington, IN 47403
www.westbowpress.com
1 (866) 928-1240

ISBN: 978-1-5127-9117-4 (sc)
ISBN: 978-1-5127-9116-7 (hc)
ISBN: 978-1-5127-9118-1 (e)

Library of Congress Control Number: 2017909634

Print information available on the last page.

WestBow Press rev. date: 06/19/2017

This book is dedicated to Mike
and Ruth Hryshkanych.

Thank you for showing me what living a godly life
is like and what a godly relationship looks like.

Chapter 1

It was the middle of December, and all around it looked like a winter wonderland. Everything was covered in snow. As Raelynn looked out the car window, she was amazed at the sight. When she got out and approached the cottage, the snow began to lightly fall around her.

The cottage was set back in the woods of northern Wisconsin and had a mile-long driveway. This was her favorite time of the year. She had always spent Christmas break at the cottage with her family. It had been her little hideaway from the real world.

Raelynn had come here for the first time when she was a young child. Over time, the cottage had become a little run-down, but her father could fix anything. On the outside, the cottage looked small and like it was made from logs. Inside, the ground floor had a small living space, kitchen, and a full bathroom. The upstairs had only three bedrooms. Over the years, her parents had remodeled the bedrooms to make them larger.

Her absolute favorite part of the cottage was the wooden railing that ran along the side of the stairs. It looked just like someone had taken the bark right off the tree, resized it, and put it in the cottage.

It had been a few Christmases since her entire family had been there. For the past few years, Raelynn and her parents had been the only ones there. This year, her older brother, Gavin, was bringing his wife, Joyelle, and their two sons. It felt a little odd to Raelynn that there would be more than just the four of them this year but loved the idea of packing more people into her favorite place.

Her parents had moved to the cottage a few years ago because they had not wanted to stay in downtown

Milwaukee. They had always loved the cottage and had wanted to start a new life there when they retired.

Even though Raelynn loved to visit the cottage, she never saw herself living in that area. She had always loved city life so had decided to attend Hardin Valley University (HVU) in Greeneville, Tennessee. It had been quite a move from Milwaukee to Greeneville, but she had enjoyed every minute of it.

Hardin Valley was a huge school and was where all the famous artists went. She aspired to become the next best painter and was in her fourth year of college. She really loved living in Tennessee and planned to stay there awhile after she graduated. Some of her work was already in a Greeneville art gallery and some was in the fine arts building.

She had made many friends while attending HVU. Most of them were not artists, but she loved the fact that they didn't share everything in common.

Raelynn got out of the car and was greeted by her two loving parents. Her father, John, reminded her of what she used to think Santa Claus looked like. He had a snow-white beard and a round stomach. He was almost bald but refused to think so. He was looking forward to dressing up like Santa for Gavin's sons, Garrett and Gideon. Raelynn was now just as tall as her father at five feet, eleven inches, and her mother was only three inches shorter. Her mother, Donna, always reminded Raelynn of her grandmother: sweet, kind, and caring. Her mother was slim and had finally accepted the fact that she was getting gray hair.

"Hi, Mom! Hi, Dad! I've missed you," Raelynn exclaimed as her parents hugged and kissed her.

Her mother replied, "Raelynn, Dear, it is good to see you. We have missed you so much."

"We were worried you weren't going to make it for Christmas this year, but we are glad that you did," her dad stated.

Raelynn smiled and asked her father for help with her luggage. When they got inside, she moved into her room.

After she settled in, they sat around the fireplace and drank coffee. Raelynn and her parents talked about school and her future. They talked about her plans to stay in Tennessee after she graduated. They talked about family news and her parents' new home. Raelynn enjoyed having this time with her parents. They were having a nice conversation. It had been so long since she had sat down and just talked about life with her parents. Everything was going smoothly until her mother brought up the topic of boys.

Raelynn hated to talk about guys. Her schooling was so intense, she didn't have time to date. On top of her schooling, she was about to get an internship under Reagan Dimes, an artist who worked at the local art gallery in Greeneville. Reagan had told her that she was promising, which was how her work got into the gallery. She was really looking forward to learning the ropes of the art world under Reagan Dimes.

Raelynn's mom said, "Have you found a guy yet? You really should be more involved in extracurricular activities instead of locking yourself up in your room."

"Mom, you know that I don't have time for those kinds of things. All I have time for is homework and church," Raelynn replied.

"I keep telling your mother not to worry about you. We know that the right guy will come along when it's time," her father said.

Just as Raelynn started to defend herself, they heard her brother's car pull up the driveway. Raelynn jumped up and ran outside to greet them. She thought their timing could not have been more perfect. She felt so relieved.

"Hi, everybody! Oh, I've missed you so very much!" Joyelle said as she went to give Raelynn a hug. Garrett and Gideon jumped out of the car and ran to hug their grandparents as Gavin walked over to his sister. Many hugs were given out, and there was much commotion.

After all the hugs and hellos were finished, they carried the luggage in, and Gavin and his family were given a chance to get settled.

Later, Joyelle and Raelynn helped with dinner while

the boys hung out in the living room. Raelynn's mother was almost finished making the meal so they helped with the final touches. The boys talked about school and their friends. Gavin talked about his new job promotion. Their father caught them up to speed on things that had been going on around the house.

While in the kitchen, Joyelle and Raelynn shared about what had been going on in their lives. Raelynn told Joyelle all about classes at college and her new job opportunity. Joyelle told Raelynn all about her boys starting first grade and about Gavin's work promotion. Their mother listened and then filled them in on the new things that had been improved in the house. Raelynn was glad they were able to talk and be together as a family.

For dinner, they were having ham, mashed potatoes, green beans, grape salad, and gravy. Their grandmother knew that Garrett and Gideon loved the grape salad, which was why she had decided to make it this year. For dessert, they had peach cobbler and ice cream. Raelynn and Gavin's mother always went out of their way when she had company over. This came as no surprise to them. They were glad to eat their mother's food.

"Mom, this looks delicious. You have really outdone yourself," Gavin said as they all sat down to eat.

"I told your mother that she didn't have to do this tonight, but she would not listen to me. In fact, I'm so hungry I'm glad she made all this," their father said and then laughed.

As Donna set the last dish down, the rest of the family came to the table and found their seats. Everyone joined hands around the table except for Garrett and Gideon. The boys started to reach for the food, but their mother quickly stopped them. Joyelle kindly reminded them that they still had to pray and were not to dish up the food until afterward. John asked Gavin to pray for dinner and then closed his eyes.

They bowed their heads and closed their eyes. Gavin began to pray, "Dear Lord, thank you for all the wonderful food that we are about to eat. Bless the hands that have prepared the meal. I pray that we all would enjoy this weekend together before heading back to school. Thank you for allowing us to come and join our family to celebrate the birth of your Son. Amen."

As soon as Gavin finished his prayer, they passed the food. Conversations filled the dining room and love flooded the cottage. They were all glad to be with each other and to eat a home-cooked meal. It had been about two months since Raelynn had eaten a nice, homemade meal. She had not been able to make it home at Thanksgiving due to an art show, so she was grateful that she could make it home for Christmas.

After they finished dinner, they decided that they were too full to eat the peach cobbler, which Donna had made. Garret and Gideon helped their grandmother clear the table and load the dishwasher while Donna put the food away. John made a pot of coffee, and everyone but the twins grabbed a cup. Once everything had been cleaned up and everyone had a cup of coffee, they went into the living room.

Garrett and Gideon sat on the couch by their parents. They played games on their tablets while the grown-ups talked. Gavin and Joyelle went and grabbed blankets from the closet because the heating in the cottage was not working very well. Donna and John both sat in their comfy chairs, and Raelynn sat in the rocking chair.

They talked about their plans for the weekend. The twins found out that the cottage did not have Wi-Fi, so they wouldn't be able to watch their favorite Netflix show until they got home. They had all been so excited to be together again that they had not remembered some of the regular precautions they normally took. Everybody was happy and the room was filled with laughter when, suddenly, the power went out.

Chapter 2

"We blew the breaker," Gavin said as he came around the corner. "I think I've got it fixed, but we will have to see."

When the power went out it had gotten cold very quickly. Everyone had added layers of clothing and had huddled together to stay warm. John had found some flashlights and had given them to his wife and children.

"We must have had too many things plugged in," Donna stated as Joyelle and Raelynn went and checked all of the rooms.

They had found multiple space heaters with buttons in the on position, regular appliances and clocks plugged in, and the boys tablet chargers. Joyelle decided to take away the tablets for the weekend not only because of the breaker box but also because she wanted them to spend time with their grandparents and aunt.

"Boys, since there is no Wi-Fi at the cottage, we aren't going to be using our electronics for the next few days. Is that clear?" Joyelle stated.

"Yes, Mom," Garrett and Gideon replied with a melancholy tone. The boys were not happy about this decision but decided not to back talk because they knew that would get them into trouble.

Gavin and Joyelle went around the house and unplugged unnecessary items, John got more logs for the fireplace, Donna found a space heater, and the boys went into the living room. They started to talk to each other about what they thought they might get for Christmas but stopped talking as soon as Raelynn came in and sat in the rocking chair.

"Wow! You boys sure got quiet quickly," Raelynn said.

"We weren't talking about anything, Aunt Raelynn," Garrett said as he smiled mischievously at his brother.

"Somehow, I don't believe you two," Raelynn replied.

Garrett and Gideon started to laugh and then made her promise not to tell their parents. She promised not to tell, and the boys started to fill her in on what they had previously been talking about—what they wanted for Christmas. Raelynn laughed at what they had been hiding but then took it very seriously when she saw that they were not kidding around. She told them not to mess around with the presents once they were under the tree.

Gideon asked, "Will our mom and dad find out?"

Raelynn said, "Well, they might hear you get up. You would probably be in trouble if they found out. And you don't want to risk not getting any gifts."

The boys agreed with their aunt, and they ended that conversation as the rest of the family came in. Joyelle told the boys to get ready for bed and that she would be up in five short minutes. They raced upstairs to see who would reach the bedroom first. Garrett reached the top of the staircase first and shouted, "I win!" Then they rushed to their room and got ready for bed.

"Don't forget to brush your teeth," Joyelle yelled up the stairs to the boys.

As the adults gathered in the living room, they discussed their plans for the next few days. They talked about the meals and the activities they would do. They talked about Christmas Eve and Christmas day. They talked about how to keep Garrett and Gideon busy.

Joyelle went upstairs and found her two boys waiting patiently for her. Before she tucked them in and said good night, they all prayed together. Garrett and Gideon loved to pray before going to bed. It was their favorite part of the day. Joyelle sat down on the floor while the boys climbed up onto the air mattress and sat on top of the blankets. Just as they were about ready to pray, Gavin walked in and sat next to his wife.

"You didn't think I'd miss this, did you?" Gavin said to his boys.

Gideon said, "No, I didn't. I heard you coming up the stairs." They all laughed. Once the boys calmed down, Joyelle prayed, Gideon and Garrett each took a turn, and then Gavin closed. They tucked the boys into bed, turned off the lights, and went downstairs.

Gideon and Garrett talked about building snowmen and snow forts. They talked about having a snowball fight and how much fun it would be. By the time they finished their conversation, they were so excited for the next morning to come, they had a hard time falling asleep. They thought they heard their parents coming upstairs so they lay down and pretended to be asleep. Their parents did not come upstairs, but the boys fell asleep anyway.

As it got later, Donna and John went to bed. Gavin went up to check on the boys but ended up going to bed. Raelynn made more coffee while Joyelle locked up the cottage for the night.

Joyelle took a seat on the couch, and Raelynn came in with a hot mug of coffee in each hand. She placed one on the table in front of Joyelle and then seated herself next to her sister-in-law.

"So how has school really been?" Joyelle asked.

"It's been okay. I'm ready to get my last year done and hopefully get an internship. I have a pretty good shot at the gallery," Raelynn replied.

"Well, that's cool. I hope that you can get some more work published. An internship there would be great for you."

Raelynn nodded her agreement.

"Now I know that you don't really like to talk about this but is there any significant other in your life right now?"

"Honestly, no there isn't. I haven't really had time for a relationship these past few years. I've been so focused on school and getting my work published that I haven't really had much of a social life. I kind of wish that I had made time for a social life and had met someone, but it hasn't happened yet."

"I know how you feel. It was like that for me before I met your brother. Have I ever told you that story?"

"No, I don't think you have. I know you told me about how he proposed but not how you met. Can I hear it?"

"It was the start of our senior year in college. I had just transferred into Central Valley. I decided to go to this thing called Block Bash. All the different clubs on campus got together and tried to recruit people to come to their events. I was walking down the sidewalk and decided to take a look at the CRU stand. That's when I met Gavin. He was handing out flyers for CRU. He was one of the leaders that year. I immediately fell for him."

Raelynn stopped her, "How did you know he was the person you wanted to date?"

"I don't really know. I think that it was the fact that he was so on fire for God. It's a really attractive characteristic."

"Okay, go on."

"We started talking, mostly about CRU. I decided to check it out because I wanted to be involved in some activity my last year. So when I showed up on Thursday night, your brother and one of the other leaders were greeting people at the door. I said hi and slid past him into one of the back rows. He was giving the message

"I like to think so," Joyelle laughed, "but there were and still are times that it doesn't feel like a fairytale. We were both ready for a relationship, and I think that that helped. As long as we keep our eyes focused on God and serving each other before ourselves, we do all right."

"Is it hard putting each other first?"

"Sometimes, it's really a struggle when I want to take a nap after a long day with the boys but have to make dinner. There are days when I just want to be by myself but know that I need to stay up and talk to Gavin when he gets home. We all have those selfish motives, and they can get in the way of loving God and serving our spouses."

They talked until 1:00 a.m. and then decided they should go to bed. They washed out their mugs, turned off the lights, grabbed their blankets, and walked upstairs. They stopped when they got to the top of the staircase and gave each other a hug before entering their rooms.

"I'll be praying for you that God brings someone into your life," Joyelle whispered.

"Thank you. I'll be praying for you and your family too," Raelynn replied softly.

They opened and closed their doors quietly, trying not to wake anyone up. Joyelle crawled into bed next to her husband and kissed him on the forehead before lying down.

Raelynn wasn't tired at all. Her mind was spinning with crazy thoughts. She got ready for bed and then organized her room. She was going through her suitcase when she came across her Bible. She realized she hadn't read it in the past few days and decided to do it right then. She read a few chapters in the books of Psalm and Proverbs and then ended with James.

She had missed her time with God. She was glad she had decided to spend time with Him. She had been feeling spiritually dry until she read her Bible. She thought it was amazing how God's Word could fill you up. She ended her time with God in prayer.

She prayed, "Dear Father, I pray that I will continue to follow You and Your will for me. You are all I need in this life. Please help me to see that. If You do have a spouse and a family for me in Your plan, that would be wonderful. But if not, help me to be okay with that. Help me to keep my focus on You and living my life for You. Help me to love and serve others. Help my artwork to point to You. May it be all for Your glory. I pray for my family members. Help them to love others and to love You. I pray this all in Your name. Amen."

She placed her Bible on her dresser, got an extra blanket, and then crawled into bed. She turned off the light. She tossed and turned for a long time and then turned the light back on. She could not get her mind to stop thinking about all the different outcomes that could occur in her life. She finally decided to give it all to God again. She turned out the light and lay in bed praying until she fell asleep. It worked. Soon she was asleep but had forgotten to set her alarm.

Chapter 3

Raelynn hadn't needed an alarm to wake her up the next morning. Her nephews had done a fine job of that. They had jumped up and down on her bed and yelled that breakfast was ready. She had woken up within a few seconds and had told them that she would be downstairs in a couple of minutes.

As she got dressed for the day in her usual sweatpants and favorite navy-blue sweatshirt and topped it off with a messy bun, she could hear the clatter of dishes and silverware as the table was being set. The cottage was full of commotion, and it was only eight in the morning.

When she reached the bottom of the stairs, her family was just sitting down at the table. Her family members greeted her with warm smiles. She poured herself a cup of coffee and took her seat.

After John prayed, they passed around the food. Her mother's egg casserole was her favorite breakfast food. Raelynn always loved waking up to the smell of this casserole when she visited. The casserole was accompanied by bacon, sausage, and a variety of breakfast drinks. They all enjoyed the food but did not say much. They were either so tired or hungry that no one wanted to talk.

Once breakfast ended, Gavin and Joyelle washed the dishes while the rest of the family cleared the food from the table. They got refills on hot chocolate and coffee and then went to the living room.

Raelynn thought that Garrett and Gideon had too much energy for nine o'clock in the morning. She knew that being up too late the night before was making her feel groggy. She stared at the wall and sipped her hot coffee. She was glad that she had put on her wool socks, because there was a chill lingering in the air.

Raelynn scanned the room and evaluated everyone's energy level. Her nephews had the highest level while her brother and parents seemed normal. When she got to her sister-in-law, she laughed. Joyelle looked exhausted. After going to bed late and having two energetic young boys, Raelynn could not even imagine how drained Joyelle must be.

Joyelle caught Raelynn's eye and smiled at her. John and Gavin seemed to be having a great conversation while the boys played with their action figures. Donna was listening attentively to the conversation. Raelynn and Joyelle just watched everything happen around them.

"Raelynn, would you like a refill?" Gavin said while snapping his fingers in front of Raelynn's eyes.

She nodded her head and replied with a kind and gentle, "Yes, please."

"You and Joyelle seem really out of it this morning," Gavin said as he took her cup and Raelynn nodded. She could not believe how tired and exhausted she felt. It had been a while since she had felt this way.

When Gavin came back into the room, he handed Raelynn her coffee. She took a sip and was a little surprised that he had remembered exactly how she liked it. She smiled.

"Is it all right?" Gavin questioned.

"Yes, it's perfect. Exactly how I like it. Thank you," Raelynn said.

"Daddy, can I try some of your coffee?" Garrett asked. "I've always wanted to know what it tastes like."

Gavin handed him the cup and both of his boys took a large sip.

"Yuck!" "Gross!" Garrett and Gideon shouted as they ran to get a drink of water.

"What was wrong with the coffee? Did you not like it?" Joyelle asked her sons when they walked back into the room.

"It tasted yucky. I'm never having that again!" Gideon said.

"It's black. My favorite," Gavin said as he showed his family the mug. They all laughed.

It was about noon when they finished their coffee and lounge around time. They had sandwiches and leftover grape salad for lunch. During the meal, Garrett and Gideon talked their aunt into going outside and building a snow fort. Raelynn figured she could play with her nephews for a while. She thought her brother and sister-in-law would be grateful to have some time without the boys.

The boys ran upstairs to get their snow clothes on. It took them only a matter of minutes and then they were out the door. The boys ran outside first, but Raelynn was not far behind them. As she walked out the door, Joyelle looked at her, smiled, and whispered a thank-you.

Garrett and Gideon piled up the snow for their fort's foundation. They wanted the fort to be something extravagant. They didn't get much snow where they lived in California.

Raelynn was not used to having this much snow. Sometimes, work and school were cancelled when too much snow fell. But not much snow was needed to cause the closings. She loved where she lived. She wouldn't trade it for anything but also loved coming home to more snow than the southern states would ever see.

Raelynn smiled and laughed at her nephews. They were adorable, loved playing together, and especially loved being outside. Once their fort was completed, they took a step back to look at their masterpiece.

"It's beautiful," Garrett said in amazement as he and his brother stared at the fort.

Raelynn smiled while saying, "It sure is. You did a great job."

She hugged them both. They were cold so they decided to go inside and to warm up.

They took their wet snow clothes off by the door and ran upstairs to put on something dry. Raelynn changed back into what she had worn that morning because it was really warm and comfortable.

Joyelle had coffee and hot chocolate ready to pour when the boys came back downstairs. The boys sat down at the table and sipped their hot chocolate. They were thankful their mom knew how to make it just right and told her so. Raelynn slid onto a barstool at the kitchen's small island. Joyelle passed her a cup of coffee and the fixings for it. Raelynn thanked her and fixed her coffee to her liking. Before she knew it, the rest of the family had joined them in the dining area.

Garrett and Gideon told everyone how they had built the fort and about all the fun they had had. They told everyone how they had chased Raelynn through the snow, and she had fallen, so they had piled on top of her. They talked about their snowball fight they had had halfway through building their snow fort. They told everyone how amazed they had been when they had finished. The family laughed with them as they shared. Raelynn missed times like these. She was sad that they all lived so far apart.

They had dinner early. After that, the boys made Christmas candy with their grandparents. Raelynn was able to catch up a little bit with her brother and his wife, but her nephews kept interrupting.

When the candy was finished, they all moved to the living room. Gideon and Garrett wanted to play in the snow some more. They got ready and ran outside to play.

Gavin, Joyelle, and Raelynn decided to ambush the boys with snowballs. They got dressed in their winter gear and snuck outside. They made the snowballs and then charged the fort. Garrett and Gideon were quick to retaliate. The adults soon realized the bad choice they had made. They had forgotten that the boys could take cover behind their fort. It was late when they finally came back inside laughing.

"It looked like you were all having fun out there," Donna said as she invited them into the kitchen for warm drinks.

"Oh, we were, Grandma!" Garrett said.

"Next time you should come out there with us," Gideon stated.

"Maybe we will join you, but that will take some convincing," John said.

They drank their hot chocolate and coffee and, one

As the day continued, they opened more presents. Raelynn had come to the conclusion that she would not need anything for a while. She knew her small apartment wouldn't hold much more stuff.

They laughed and talked into the evening. The boys went to bed, and for the last time that weekend, the adults were able to have some time alone.

As the evening grew later and later, Donna and John went to bed. It was close to eleven o'clock, and they weren't used to staying up very late. They were so glad that their small family had been close to them again.

Gavin, Joyelle, and Raelynn were the only ones still up. They talked about Raelynn possibly coming to visit them over spring break. Raelynn needed to check with the gallery but was sure she could get off. She really wanted to be more involved in her nephews' lives.

Once midnight struck, Joyelle went to bed. She knew her boys would be up early and needed to be ready to cope with their energy and the long drive to the airport.

Gavin and Raelynn finally got the sibling time they had been waiting for. Even though Gavin was almost five years older than she was, they were still close. Because there were only two of them, they were a big part of one another's lives. They were at different places in their lives but that did not divide them too much.

Gavin and Raelynn talked until almost three in the morning. Then they decided to get some rest, knowing they both had long drives ahead of them. They hugged each other and went to their rooms. It wasn't long before Raelynn was asleep.

Chapter 4

As they loaded the last bags into their cars, tears were forming in the corners of their eyes. They could not believe how quickly the past week had gone by. Raelynn was not looking forward to going back to work in the next couple of days but was grateful for the time she had been able to spend with her family. Hugs were given and plans for their next visit started to form.

Raelynn helped Garrett and Gideon get into their car and made sure they were buckled up. Before they got in, her nephews gave her a kiss on each cheek and another big hug. They asked her if she would visit them soon, and she said that she hoped too.

Gavin and his family were the first to leave. They

waved as they headed down the driveway. Raelynn was sad to see them go but knew she had to leave as well. Raelynn put her purse and water bottle in the front passenger's seat of her car and shut the door. She turned around to give her parents one more hug before she began her long journey back to Tennessee.

After hugging her parents, Raelynn left for home. She had about a twelve-hour drive home. Thankfully, it was only eight o'clock in the morning so she wouldn't get back too late. She was glad she would only have to drive one day, although her brother only had to drive to the airport.

As she drove through Wisconsin, Illinois, part of Kentucky, and finally Tennessee, she couldn't help but think about what her parents had said to her the night she had arrived at the cottage. She thought, *Why am I the only one of my friends who is single? I'm twenty-two. I should have found someone by now.*

The more Raelynn thought about it, the more upset she became. God had a plan and knew what He was doing. She didn't know what that plan for her was yet but continued to trust Him.

Raelynn pulled into a parking space by her apartment complex and turned her car off. She grabbed her things and walked up the stairs to her apartment. She opened the door and went in. Raelynn took off her coat and boots and hung her keys up. She dragged her stuff to her room. When she came back out to make some coffee, her roommate, Claire, arrived.

They were very excited to be together again. Both of them had gone home for the holidays and hadn't seen each other for a few weeks.

"Raelynn! I'm so happy to see you!" Claire said as she ran across the kitchen to hug Raelynn.

"Claire! Oh am I happy to see you! I have so much to tell you about my trip," Raelynn said as she hugged her friend.

Claire had blond hair, which was so light it looked like it had been bleached. Her blue eyes were always a conversation piece. They were so bright there was no way you could miss them.

Claire took her stuff to her room and got settled. Raelynn made coffee. Once Claire was done she joined Raelynn on the couch for some coffee and a chat. Claire and Raelynn had been roommates and best friends since their freshman year. This was their fourth year together. Their degrees were taking them longer than they had hoped, but they loved living together.

"How was your vacation? You are so fortunate to have been able to get off of work for the whole month," Raelynn said as Claire took a seat.

"It was really good. I got to spend a lot of time with my family and other family members who I don't get to see very often. So that was nice. My older sister and her boyfriend announced their engagement a few days before Christmas. She asked me to be her maid of honor, and I got excited about the wedding. We are going to start planning it soon," Claire said.

"That is so exciting for both of you! I'm happy for your sister," Raelynn said.

Claire continued, "Thanks. I'm glad I have a lighter

class load next semester. I am kind of looking forward to going back to work. I miss my work friends. Anyway, enough about me. How was your break? You said you had stuff to tell me."

"Where do I start?" Raelynn laughed. "Well, my parents questioned my relationship status again."

"Oh, no. You know that they are just concerned about you, and they love you."

"I know. It's hard, sometimes, to see that. But I got to have a nice long chat with Joyelle the first night and one with Gavin the last night. That was really nice, and I needed it. I got to spend a lot of time outside in the snow with Garrett and Gideon. We built a fort and had multiple snowball fights. It was great."

They both laughed. Raelynn continued to talk about all the crazy events that she and her family had encountered that weekend. She started with the power outage and then told about Garret and Gideon's Wi-Fi withdrawals. They reminisced about the entire vacation until midnight. Then they locked up the apartment and headed to their rooms.

The next day was Raelynn's last day off and then she would start work. Thankfully, it would be a Monday, so it would be the start of a brand new week.

She lay in bed awake for a while. Her mind raced. Raelynn kept thinking about her singleness. At about three in the morning, she decided enough was enough and prayed that she wouldn't worry about it anymore. She fell asleep at around four o'clock and was exhausted by the time sleep finally came.

The next morning, Raelynn woke up to the smell of coffee. It was a little past ten o'clock when she decided to get up for the day. She walked to the kitchen so she could put some coffee into her system and wake herself up. Claire was at the counter reading her Bible and drinking coffee.

"Morning, roomie," Claire said as Raelynn slowly entered the kitchen.

"Morning," Raelynn replied while pouring herself a cup of coffee.

Raelynn walked into their living room with her coffee and sat on the couch. She stared at the TV. Claire could tell that Raelynn was still half asleep, so she decided to give her time to wake up and went back to her reading.

After her cup of coffee, Raelynn was awake and ready to eat breakfast. She decided to have some cereal and joined Claire at the counter.

"How did you sleep last night?" Claire asked and then pointed out that it looked like it had been a rough night for Raelynn.

"I had trouble falling asleep and then staying asleep," Raelynn replied.

They talked about their plans for the day and what the next few days would look like. Raelynn told Claire that she would probably watch Netflix all day and go to bed early. She wanted to order Chinese takeout for dinner. Claire agreed on dinner. She said she was planning on visiting work for a little bit and then would be at the apartment all day.

As Claire got ready to leave, Raelynn got dressed

and then did some laundry. After Claire left, Raelynn made herself comfortable on the couch with multiple blankets and pillows. She went and got another cup of coffee. She picked up the TV remote and went to Netflix. Raelynn quickly put on *Friends*, her favorite show, and relaxed.

Claire came home about four hours later. She had had a lot of errands to run after visiting work. Raelynn had just paused the episode to finish her laundry when Claire walked in. Claire ordered their takeout dinner and then joined Raelynn in the living room.

Thirty minutes later, they both jumped when they heard the knock on the door. It was their dinner. Claire ran to the door with money to pay for it, and Raelynn paused the show. They went to the kitchen counter and transferred their food to plates and grabbed something to drink. They returned to the living room with their food and continued to watch their show.

Around nine o'clock that night, Raelynn decided to get some sleep. She helped Claire clean up the living room and did the dishes. She took a quick shower before heading to bed.

By ten o'clock, she was in bed and hoped she would sleep well. As Raelynn dosed off, she heard Claire on the phone with what sounded like Claire's boyfriend, Jaden, in the other room. Raelynn fell asleep quickly.

The next morning, she was startled when her alarm went off. She couldn't believe it was already time to get up and get ready, but she did anyway.

When she was ready, she poured some coffee into her travel mug and headed out the door. It was starting to snow lightly, and she walked slowly to her car so she wouldn't slip and fall.

She drove to work and was greeted by Reagan Dimes, her boss. As they walked to her office, Reagan told her about everything that had happened while she was gone. Raelynn was surprised at how happy her coworkers were to see her. Raelynn and Reagan discussed her school schedule and how she would work around it. Afterward, she walked out to her desk and began her day.

Chapter 5

"Hello, I'm just wondering if you have any paintings by Leonid Afremov," the young man said.

"Um, I think so. Hold on. Let me look them up and then I can show you where they are," Raelynn said.

"Thank you."

"It looks like we do have quite a few paintings by Mr. Afremov. Right this way." Raelynn guided the young man toward the foyer and down the hallway.

"My name is Brady, Brady Jones."

"Hi, it's nice to meet you. I'm Raelynn Blake."

"How long have you worked here?"

"I just started in October. I got an internship here under Mrs. Dimes."

"Oh, that's cool."

"Yeah," Raelynn said. "Well, here's his exhibit. If you need any other help, you know where my desk is."

"Oh, thank you."

Raelynn turned around and walked back to her desk. She sat down and saw that she had a few messages. She listened to and returned the calls. She had a lot of emails to process and a bunch of distributers and donators to get in contact with. When Brady walked back toward her desk, she was so busy she didn't notice him standing there. She was on the phone with a donator and was having a very interesting conversation.

"Yes, sir. No, we have not received that yet. I will let you know when we have. Yes, sir. No, sir. Okay. Would you like me to transfer you to Mrs. Dimes? Okay, I'll transfer you. Have a good day."

Then Raelynn looked up and saw Brady standing in front of her desk, "Oh, hi there. Is there anything else you needed?"

"No. I just wanted to thank you. I'll see you around. Bye."

"My pleasure. Have a good day."

Raelynn smiled. Brady smiled back, turned, and left. Raelynn quickly got back to work. She could not believe how busy the day had been. Raelynn was thankful when Reagan buzzed her over the phone system. Raelynn got up, grabbed a pen and notepad, and walked to Reagan's office. She knocked on her office door, and Reagan told her to come in.

"You wanted to see me?" Raelynn asked.

"Yes. Have a seat," Reagan replied.

Raelynn sat down in the chair across from Reagan. Reagan seemed to have something on her mind. It worried Raelynn. She could not remember the last time she had seen Reagan so discombobulated.

"Is everything okay?" Raelynn asked.

"Oh, yes. Everything is fine. How is your first day back going?"

"You sure you don't want to talk about it?"

"I'm sure. How is your day going?"

"It's been a little tough getting back into the swing of things, but it's going well."

"I'm really glad that your day is going well. I just wanted to go over a few details with you for the new wing that is opening next weekend."

"All right, I'm listening." Raelynn smiled and got her pen and notepad ready.

For the next hour and a half, Raelynn and Reagan discussed the opening of the new wing. They talked about what kinds of appetizers and drinks they would serve. They had decided not to have this event catered because last time it had gone badly. The caterers hadn't prepared the food correctly and hadn't brought what they had requested. They planned to serve finger sandwiches with chips and dip, water, lemonade, and iced tea. Reagan didn't like to serve any champagne at her events because she wanted her guests to be able to respect the art. Reagan put Raelynn in charge of finding a wide ribbon for the ribbon-cutting ceremony. They decided to go with a classic red-ribbon color.

When they had finished their discussion, it was the end of the workday. Raelynn clocked out, gathered her belongings, said goodbye to her coworkers, and walked to her car. On her way home, she remembered how much she hated rush hour, so she turned on her radio. She picked up pizza for her and her roommate's dinner.

Raelynn unlocked the apartment door and went in. She set the food on the counter and called for Claire, but there was no answer. She checked her phone. There were no messages. She texted Claire that she was at home and had Chinese food. Claire replied that she would be home shortly.

Raelynn changed into sweats and warmed up the Chinese food. She made up two plates and set them on the coffee table. She turned on the news to catch up on life in Greeneville.

Claire arrived, greeted Raelynn, and went to her room to change. Claire emerged from her bedroom in sweatpants and a hoodie and sat down by Raelynn. She thanked her for dinner. They ate and talked about their busy days. As the theme song to their favorite show began, Raelynn asked Claire about her day.

"How was your day, Claire?" Raelynn asked.

"It was pretty good. Work was slow, so I accomplished many tasks. I had a lot of paperwork to do and to file. I was happy that my boss didn't have any extra projects. I was able to get a lot of my secretarial work done. I had emails to read and reply to. There was more work to do as the day went on. More emails and paperwork came through after I got back from lunch," Claire said.

"Wow. It does sound like you were busy. I'm glad your boss didn't assign you extra projects today," Raelynn replied.

"Yeah. Anyway, how was your day?" Claire asked.

"It was really good. I got a lot done and caught up on all of my paperwork, emails, and filing. Reagan and I finished planning the grand opening of the new wing. That took us a few hours. Someone came in today to look at the art, so that made my day interesting. He asked to see a painter that isn't that well-known, so I had to look him up in our system."

Claire said, "Oh, really? What did he look like? Was he cute? What was he wearing?"

Raelynn stared at her friend. "Well, I didn't particularly find him attractive, but he looked nice. He was probably about six foot three and had dark-brown hair and blue-green eyes. He was wearing dark washed jeans and tennis shoes. He had an olive-green shirt on with a light jean jacket over it and a guitar slung over his back."

"What's his name? Did you talk much? I want all the details."

"Like I've told you a million times before, I'm not looking for a boyfriend right now, Claire. We talked as I showed him the artwork. His name is Brady. He goes to school here at HVU, but I don't remember what he said his major was. He said he's only into art that reflects music, so I'm guessing he's some type of musician. He spoke to me before he left, but other than that, we didn't talk much. After I showed him the art, I went back to my desk and kept working. He was different ... in a good way. I think we would be friends if I knew him better."

"Oh, okay. This Brady guy sounds like a cool dude. I hope he comes into the museum again so you guys can talk. Or maybe you'll see him around campus!" Claire smiled and winked at her roommate.

Raelynn rolled her eyes, "I don't think that's going to happen. HVU is fairly big, and there are a lot of people who go there. The chances of us running into each other on campus is very slim. I don't think that we'll see each other anytime soon. I'll only see him again if he comes into the museum."

They continued to talk as they watched a few more episodes of their TV show. Around 11:30 p.m., they cleaned up the food and dishes and got ready for bed. As they walked to their rooms, they said goodnight to each other. Raelynn turned her light off and climbed into bed.

As she set her alarm, her mind began to race. Raelynn knew that Claire would keep pestering her about Brady but that nothing would happen with him. She definitely was not going to tell her parents because they would freak out and run with it. Raelynn decided to keep any further interactions with this boy and any other boy to herself unless she knew it could lead somewhere.

Chapter 6

The next morning, Raelynn woke up and got ready for work. She was quickly getting back into the routine of what she liked to call a normal life. In all actuality, her life was filled with chaos. Somehow, she managed. She quickly straightened her long nutmeg-brown hair while staring herself down in the mirror. She thought that her eyes looked tired, and it made her drowsy. If she could change anything about herself, it would be her eyes. She always wanted bright-blue eyes but was stuck with dark-brown ones. She had tried colored contacts, but they did not look natural. She brushed her hair and turned the flat iron off. She put on her tights and a black dress, pulled on her coat, and headed out the door.

She got on the highway at just the right time and missed the morning traffic. She went through the Starbucks drive-through and bought some coffee. She was very fortunate that Starbucks wasn't very far from the gallery. She arrived at work, parked, and hastily walked inside.

She sat down at her desk and punched in. She was a minute early. She had barely made it, but that was okay. Reagan still hadn't arrived. She double-checked the parking lot as she ran in. Reagan did not like it when employees were late and had a strict policy against it. Raelynn had never seen or heard of anyone getting into trouble. It was probably due to the fact that everyone made sure they were there on time. Raelynn quickly logged into her email and began to work. She always tried to be working before Reagan got there.

It was almost lunchtime before Reagan got to the gallery. She was unpredictable but was also the boss, so no one said anything. Raelynn greeted her when she arrived. Reagan motioned for Raelynn to follow her that night. He talked about loving God and loving others. He talked about how we serve others and serve God. It was a great message, but I couldn't get over the fact that he kept looking my way. I blushed several times.

"Afterward he came and talked to me. I was almost out the door, but he caught me just in time. He asked if he could get to know me better. I said yes. We went on many dates just to get to know each other before we became girlfriend and boyfriend. My roommate also attended CRU with me, so we talked about your brother a lot.

"By the end of our time in college, we had been dating for about a year and a half. We both had to do an extra semester and internship. We had met each other's families and had fallen in love with them. When he met my family, he asked my parents for my hand in marriage. A few months later, Gavin proposed. And that's the story of how we met."

"Wow, that's so cool! I'm glad that you told me that story. It sounds like a fairytale."

by one, went off to bed. Raelynn and Joyelle stayed behind after everyone went upstairs. It was their turn to lock up. It was so late nobody was up to talking. They locked and secured the cottage. They turned off the lights and walked up the staircase to their rooms.

By the time they got upstairs, everyone was in his or her room, and it was quiet. Joyelle and Raelynn sat on the top step and talked for a little while. They had to whisper because the rooms were right around the corner. It was about a half an hour later when they went to bed. Raelynn was so thankful to have a wonderful sister-in-law.

The next few days flew by. When she woke on Christmas morning, Raelynn was surprised that her mini-vacation was almost over. She walked down the stairs and helped set the table.

Before breakfast, they decided to open their stockings. John walked around the corner dressed like Santa Claus. Garrett and Gideon were overjoyed from their grandfather pretending to be Santa.

Her first day back was going smoother than usual. She didn't want to hit any rough patches today. She answered calls and ran errands for Reagan. Claire came to visit Raelynn at lunch, and they went to the little bakery down the street.

Raelynn got back to work, and all was going well until a guy walked into the art gallery and wandered over by her desk. He was looking at the painting across from her. She thought he was about her age. She couldn't tell. Then he turned around.

into her office, so Raelynn grabbed her notebook and pen then headed in. They discussed possible upcoming projects and events.

Reagan was trying to get more people to come to the art gallery. She thought that more people needed to experience and enjoy art the way she did. She loved hosting events for the town and local celebrities. She loved finding local up-and-coming artists of all sorts and getting them into the museum. Raelynn was thankful for that, because that was how her work got into the gallery. Many other students had artwork in the gallery as well. The art gallery was constantly holding art shows for the college students and the community.

"Raelynn, I want to have a local musician perform here. I think that it would be good for us and would cause a big outcome. What do you think? We could set up a stage for the concert and sell tickets by the front door. People could also come in and buy their tickets in advance," Reagan said.

"I think that would be a really good idea. It would

be a great way for us to get more people into the gallery. We could open a few wings of the gallery so people could look around after the concert. We'd probably keep most wings closed, don't you think?" Raelynn replied.

For the next hour, they talked and planned out the concert idea. Raelynn was not completely sure how it would go but thought that it would be good for publicity. She took very detailed notes of all their plans. They finished talking, and Raelynn got up to leave. As she opened the door to leave, Reagan stopped her.

"Raelynn, before you go, I have a very specific job for you."

"Okay, what is it?"

"I want you to find a musician for the concert. It doesn't have to be anyone famous. It can be a college or high school student. The musician just has to be good. I would like this person to have a few original songs. I want him or her to have at least seven songs for the set but more would be better. Let the musician know that I will pay him or her to do this. I trust you on this."

"Okay. Are you sure you want me to do this?"

"Yes. You'll do great. Oh, and make sure to add the staff meeting to the calendar. We are having it Friday instead of Thursday."

Raelynn stood there in shock. She somehow mumbled the word, "Okay," and walked to her desk. She felt like a deer caught in the headlights. She did not know what to think. She only knew she was in way over her head. Sometimes her job had its downfalls.

Raelynn updated the staff calendar and sent out an email to remind her coworkers of the Friday evening meeting. She had a love-hate relationship with the staff meetings. She did not mind taking notes or the discussion. She loved her coworkers but hated that the meetings were at night after the gallery was closed. Most times, she wished they could come in early for the meetings but knew that Reagan wouldn't go for that idea, so she kept it to herself.

The rest of the day flew by. She spent all afternoon looking up local musicians. She had no luck. She hoped that she would run into someone at school who would meet all of Reagan's requirements and be willing to do it. She knew that getting paid would be a bonus for the musician and was glad Reagan had said that.

Everyone was packing up to head home. They shut their computers off and punched out. As Raelynn and her coworkers walked to their cars, it began to snow. It was beautiful. Raelynn loved the snow. It reminded her of her time at the cottage. She got in her car, turned the lights on, and cranked the heat to high. She pulled out onto the road and prayed that they would stay drivable until she made it back to her apartment.

She got home safely and quickly and changed into warmer and more comfortable clothing. Claire had left a note on the counter for Raelynn. It was on light-blue stationary written in black ink. Claire had the best penmanship she had seen in a long time. Raelynn loved notes from Claire because they always looked so nice. Raelynn read it as she poured herself a cup of coffee.

It said, "Hey roomie, I hope that work was good. I

got off really early. I am going out to dinner with Jaden. I should be back by ten o'clock. We promise to drive carefully because it's supposed to be icy and to snow a lot tonight. Don't worry about me. I'll text you if anything changes. See you tomorrow after class. Have a great first day back! Love, Claire."

She took the note to her bedroom and put it on her dresser. What a thoughtful thing for Claire to do. She made herself dinner and did the dishes after she ate. She decided to go to bed early. She had a class at ten the next morning but wanted to get there early so she could walk by all her classrooms. She had a short night's sleep but didn't wake up when Claire got home.

In the morning, she made sure Claire was back. She decided to look nice on her first day. For the first time in a while, she also had breakfast before school. She drove over to Hardin Valley University and parked in the commuter lot. She walked by all her classrooms and hung out in the library until 9:30 a.m. She walked to her first class, which was Introduction to Industrial Art. She did not know why she had to take it and thought it would be a boring class. She did not have a good attitude about it.

The room was large. It looked like it could hold about one hundred people. Raelynn knew that it would most likely not be a full classroom. She was right. There were about fifty people by the time class started. She sat on the end of the row about halfway down. She hated sitting in the middle. Being completely surrounded by people made her feel claustrophobic.

The professor was twenty minutes late. She was a little irritated with him because it was only a fifty-minute class. However, she didn't complain because she didn't want to be there either. Raelynn glanced around the room and thought she saw a familiar face. *No way,* she thought, *it can't be him.*

Once class ended, she deemed it an unimportant, useless class. She hated those kinds of classes. She gathered her things and got up to leave. Someone stopped her at the door. When Raelynn turned around, she was a little surprised to see Brady walking toward her.

"Hey, aren't you that girl from the art gallery?" Brady asked with a smile.

Raelynn was caught off guard. She had been right. He did look familiar.

"Um, yeah. You look familiar. I'm Raelynn. You're Brady, right?"

"Yeah! I'm Brady. I came in a few days ago to look at some art."

"Oh, yes, I remember you. Why are you taking this class?" Raelynn asked as they walked out the door into the commons area.

Brady told her that he had to take it to fulfill a requirement, and Raelynn said that that was why she was in the class too. Raelynn noticed that Brady was smiling a lot. She thought it was kind of odd, but maybe he was just a happy person. They talked for a good thirty minutes before they parted ways and headed to class.

Raelynn thought they'd had a good conversation. She smiled as she walked to her next class. She thought that something might happen between them but didn't want to get her hopes up. He seemed to like her, but she could never tell. She felt awkward in social settings but talking to Brady was different.

She quickly got rid of those thoughts from her mind. She needed to focus on school and not worry about a boy. She knew that if she told people what she was beginning to feel, they would freak out. Raelynn decided that she just wanted to be friends with Brady.

A few days passed before Brady and Raelynn talked again. She tried to avoid him, but it didn't work. They talked for another half an hour after class. Raelynn thought this might become an unhealthy habit to get into but didn't say anything. She quietly walked away and looked at the ground. She smiled and could feel herself blushing. She was frustrated she had feelings for Brady.

Stop it, Raelynn said to herself. *Focus on school, art, work, and God. You don't have time for a relationship right now.*

Chapter 7

On Raelynn's way to school, she picked up some coffee from Starbucks. She was extremely tired. She had forgotten how much sleep she needed to function in her classes. She also needed to get back into her school routine again, even though she had only been out of the routine for a month.

She got out of her car and walked to class. She saw Brady on the other side of the hallway and walked a little faster. By the time she got to class, her usual seat had been taken. She was surprises and was a little confused but sat a few rows down and on the end. Raelynn looked to her left and saw that Brady was sitting further down the same row. She quickly looked away and tried not to glance at him during the class. When class ended, she bolted for the door.

Don't make eye contact. Keep your head down. Maybe he won't see me, she thought to herself.

She was confused about why she was acting so weird. Of course, he would see her at some point because they had the same class four out of the seven days a week. Raelynn knew that she needed to get out of this funk. She had to clear her mind and refocus.

She managed to get through the rest of the day just fine. She thought that Brady might have caught on. She hoped so. He was a nice guy, but she was convinced that she didn't have time to date. Raelynn hated to hurt people's feelings and hoped that he didn't like her. If she hurt him, she would feel terrible.

The rest of the week flew by. Raelynn was so focused on school that she moved as quickly as possible from one place to the next. She was glad to get her original seat back in her the class she had with Brady. She made sure she was early every day. She saw Brady out of the corner of her eye in class but didn't focus on him.

On Friday, Brady stopped her at the door after class. She was a little surprised but took time to talk with him.

"Hey! I haven't seen you all week. How have you been?" Brady asked as he stopped Raelynn.

"Oh, hi. I've been good. Really busy. I haven't had time for much other than school or work. How are you?" Raelynn replied.

"I'm doing well. I've been trying to keep up with my homework. Trying not to stress too much."

"Oh, me too. I feel so stressed and overwhelmed, and this is only the beginning of the semester," she said, and then they both chuckled. "But my best artwork comes from when I am overwhelmed. It helps me cope."

"Really? That's so cool. The same thing happens to me with my music. Music is my stress reliever."

Brady and Raelynn talked for another fifteen minutes after class had ended. When they finished talking, Raelynn headed to her car to go to work.

She was not looking forward to her project at work. It was taking a long time to research local artists. It was a good thing her boss wasn't going to hold the concert until April. This gave her a few months to get everything planned. She was happy that she wouldn't be assigned another project until after the concert took place.

Raelynn had worked hard researching local artists the previous weekend. It was more difficult than she had originally thought it would be, and she was having no luck. She found quite a few kids from different high schools in the area who were up and coming musicians, but their parents didn't want them to perform at the gallery. She needed to find someone over the age of eighteen, but whom? She would go to all the open mikes on campus. There had to be someone at HVU who would be willing to perform.

Monday, in her Introduction to Industrial Art class, she started to zone out and to daydream. She was extremely tired because of all the research and homework she had done that weekend. She was jolted back to reality when her professor began talking about a group project. Just then, she experienced a mini anxiety attack. Raelynn hated group projects. She never did well on them. She liked projects that only included one person—herself. In most of her previous group project experiences, she had done almost all of the work. She hated that people could do close to nothing and still get the credit.

"I will put you all in groups of two. You will be required to research a theme from the industrial times and to present it in class. We will be working on these presentations all semester and won't begin presenting them until the last few weeks of the semester. Refer to the syllabus for a timeline. Once it gets closer, we will sign up for presentation days. I will pass around a sheet tomorrow for you to sign up for a theme. I do not mind if there are duplicates, but try to avoid them. Really push yourselves to research this time," Professor Barker said.

Raelynn rolled her eyes and thought, *Oh goodness, which one of these people will I get stuck with.*

Professor Barker read the names of the pairs. It

seemed completely random. She could tell he was just picking two names. As their names were called, people moved by their partners and quietly discussed what they might want to research. Everyone seemed really excited about this project.

She was even more anxious that her named hadn't been called. He surely hadn't forgotten to pair her up with someone. Although it wouldn't have been bad if he had. Some groups had three people but not hers. She froze when she heard whom she was working with. Of all people, she couldn't believe it was him.

Oh no, Raelynn thought.

"Hey there, partner. Is everything okay?" Brady asked as he sat down next to her. "I was thinking we could look at how the Industrial Revolution has affected art since we are both artists. What do you think? Raelynn? Raelynn? Hello?" Brady waved his hand in front of her face.

"I'm fine and listening. Yeah, that sounds good. Um, what's your e-mail address? This way we can add any research that we find on our own to a Google doc."

"That's a great idea! It's brady.jones@gmail.com."

"Okay. I'll create that doc tonight after work," Raelynn said as they got ready to leave class.

"Cool," Brady said and smiled. "I'll see you on Monday then."

"Bye," Raelynn quietly replied as she turned to walk to her car.

Raelynn was slightly confused and a little flustered. She called Claire as she drove to work. She needed to vent and hoped that Claire was available. She tried Claire five times, getting her voicemail each time. The last time, Raelynn left a message and told her she was headed to work but needed to talk to her when they both got home.

Work went by quickly. Raelynn tried not to let her frustration show. She worked on the project while tending to her other assistant duties. She was amazed at how well she was able to balance everything. She soon forgot about the project and had a good day.

After work, she got in her car to head home and

quickly checked her phone. A text from Claire read, "Drive safe. It's slippery. I can't wait to hear your story. P.S. I made dinner." The text caused Raelynn to have mixed emotions. She was glad to hear from her roommate, who was kind enough to make dinner, but became furious about her school project. She couldn't understand why she felt this way.

Raelynn drove very carefully on the way back to her apartment. She sat in traffic because there had been a car accident. She hoped that everyone was okay. She arrived home safely and went into the apartment. She put her stuff away and got a plate of food and glass of water.

She sat at the counter next to Claire and unloaded everything. She told her that Brady was in her class, that she had feelings for him, and how their conversation had gone. Lastly, she told Claire about her school project. Raelynn thought it was a nightmare and that nothing could make her life harder.

"What? No way! Why didn't you tell me all this before, Raelynn?" Claire asked.

"Because I knew this is how you would react. I didn't want you to get your hopes up over nothing," Raelynn said.

"Raelynn, something could happen. You never know. You need to keep an open mind. He could be a really nice guy, and you're turning him away just because you don't want a relationship? Maybe this project will help you get to know Brady better before you make a final decision. Plus you both graduate in May. Everything could change by then. Maybe nothing will change. All you have to do is be his friend and get this project done."

"You make a great point, Claire. I'll just have to wait and see what happens."

Raelynn called her parents. She hadn't spoken to them in a couple of weeks. They talked for close to an hour. They were so happy to hear from her. It made her happy to hear their voices and gave her some peace.

After the call, she went to bed more anxious than upset. She was kind of scared to see what would happen in the next few weeks but knew that everything would work itself out. She just needed to relax and refocus. Besides, what could harm her? Gaining new friends was always a good thing.

Chapter 8

The next few weeks flew by. Raelynn was keeping up with her homework. Her artwork was also coming along really well. She had a series of three paintings she was submitting to the museum over spring break in a couple of days. She had almost finished the last one and the paperwork for its submission. Raelynn was really looking forward to these new pieces being done. She loved to paint and to create things.

During spring break, Raelynn and Brady communicated by email. Things were going well with her group project. She was really surprised. She had started to get feelings again for Brady. She missed being able to talk to him in person. It was a strange feeling.

She hadn't felt like this for quite some time. Raelynn was upset that she wasn't able to get off of work to go visit her brother and his family but had a lot to do in Tennessee.

After working all break and putting the final touches on her upcoming projects, Raelynn relaxed but did not have a long time to do so. She spent all day Saturday binge watching Netflix and drinking coffee. She was glad that spring was right around the corner. This Tennessee winter had been too cold for her liking. There had been a reason she had moved to the South.

The only thing she still worried about was finding a local artist for the concert at the museum. She had all the other details planned, and everything else was set in stone ready to go for Thursday, April 23rd. Spring break had ended, and Monday rolled around.

After class, Raelynn and Brady went to one of the library's group rooms to work on their project. They were almost finished. They had just signed up for a presentation day. Both of them were very busy with school and getting ready for graduation.

"I am so looking forward to finishing this project," Raelynn said as they sat down in the room.

"Me too," Brady agreed.

"What day did you sign us up for?" Raelynn asked.

"Um, it was a Friday. Here let me check. I wrote it down." Brady thumbed through the papers in his notebook. "Oh here it is. Thursday, April 23. I hope that works for you. It's exactly a week before we graduate," Brady said.

Raelynn froze but then quickly said, "Yeah, that's fine."

"You sure?"

"Yeah, I just have a lot going on that evening. It'll be a long day."

"Oh, I'm sorry. Do you mind me asking what you've got going on?"

"Oh, no, I don't mind. I have this concert thing at the art gallery. I'm planning it with my boss. We have everything planned and ready to go. Well, all but one thing."

"What's the one thing?"

"We don't have a musician to perform for it. It kind of takes away from the whole thing. It doesn't make sense without a musician, and I cannot find one. We would pay and advertise that person. My boss wants someone who will not only do cover songs but also play originals. It would be a great experience, and they would have a large crowd. But no one seems to want to do it."

They sat in silence for a minute before Brady spoke.

"That's understandable, but I know someone who would be willing to help you out—and not because it's a paying gig."

"Anyone, please. I really need help."

"It's me. I'm the person who would be willing to help you. I have an album that will be released next summer. I would love to play at the museum. It would really help my following."

"Oh, my goodness. I totally forgot you were a musician. I cannot thank you enough. I can't wait to tell my boss. She'll be in touch with you this evening to finalize all the details. She will be so happy that we have someone."

"I'm happy to help." They both smiled.

It did not take Raelynn and Brady long to finish their project. As they were leaving, Raelynn got his cell phone number for her boss. She was so excited that she had found someone to play at the gallery.

A few days passed and then one morning Raelynn's work phone rang. She answered, and it was Brady. She was glad he had called. Raelynn was putting the finishing touches on the poster and needed a photo of him. They talked about where to hang the posters and decided that between classes on Thursday, they would go around campus and town and hang them.

Raelynn sent the ad to a few local newspapers. They planned on at least five hundred people to show up. Raelynn had even gotten Claire to hang posters up for her. Raelynn needed all the help she could get. It was going to be a very large social event. Everything was finally coming together. She could not be happier.

Raelynn had noticed that even though she and Brady had finished the project, they were still spending time together outside of class. They had sat by each other in class ever since the teacher had assigned the group project. She enjoyed being around Brady. He was really kind and caring. He loved music and God with all of his heart, and that was a rare thing to find here at HVU.

"Maybe something is happening," Raelynn thought. "I don't want to assume anything though. Maybe something will happen soon."

Brady and Raelynn spent all Thursday afternoon hanging posters up. April 23rd was only a few weeks away, and the more publicity the better.

"Are you excited to perform?" Raelynn asked as they walked down the street.

"Yeah, I am. I'm really looking forward to playing a few new originals. I think that you'll like them," Brady said.

Raelynn smiled, "Are you nervous?"

"A little."

They continued to hang up the posters and then went and grabbed a bite to eat. They had a nice conversation and a lot of laughs. Brady drove Raelynn back to HVU to get her car.

"Thanks for the ride. I really appreciate it. I had a lot of fun today," Raelynn said.

"Oh, no worries. It was my pleasure. I had a lot of fun today too," Brady replied.

There was a moment of silence between them. Then they both started to speak at the same time.

"Oh, you can go first," Brady quickly said.

"I was just going to say have a nice night," Raelynn replied. "What about you?"

"Raelynn, I have to tell you something. You don't have to say anything. But I need you to know this."

"Okay. I'm listening."

Brady began to pour his heart out, "Ever since that day when I walked into the museum, I knew that I would get to know you better. I liked you from that day on. I can't explain why, but you've never left my mind.

Being paired up with you for the project made that even clearer to me. I didn't plan it, but it happened, and I am glad that it did. I understand if you don't feel the same way, but I would really like to get to know you better. I would love to take you on a date sometime."

Raelynn did not know what to say at first but then said, "I would love to go on a date with you."

They both smiled and said goodbye. Raelynn got into her car and was extremely happy. Life kept getting better and better. She was so happy and excited for what God had in store for her.

She drove home and told Claire everything. She counted how many times Claire said, "I told you so," but that didn't matter to her anymore. She had listened to her roommate and was going on a date. Raelynn knew that Brady was an amazing guy. She slept well that night.

Chapter 9

While Raelynn curled her hair to get ready for her date with Brady, she talked to her roommate.

"Raelynn, have you decided what you want to wear tonight?" Claire asked.

"No, I haven't yet. I'm a little nervous. Should I be nervous?" Raelynn replied.

"It'll be all right. You'll have a lot of fun. You should wear your purple dress. Where are you going?"

"I'm not entirely sure. He just told me to wear a dress and that he was picking me up at seven o'clock. So I guess I'll find out soon."

Raelynn finished getting ready. She put on the purple dress and pinned her curled hair up with bobby pins.

She slid her black flats on her feet, grabbed her purse, and was ready to go by six thirty. She waited patiently with her roommate. Raelynn became nervous again, but Claire did her best to keep her calm. Raelynn was glad that she had a great friend and roommate like Claire.

Seven o'clock rolled around and was followed by a knock on their apartment door. Raelynn glanced at Claire, smiled, and went to answer the door.

Raelynn was still smiling as she opened the door and said, "Hi!"

Brady stood outside with flowers. He was wearing black dress pants with a black dress shirt and colored tie.

He smiled back and said, "Hi. Ready to go?"

Brady handed Raelynn the flowers.

"Yes, I am," Raelynn replied as she took the flowers and shut the door behind her.

Brady and Raelynn were quiet as they walked to his car. While riding to their destination, they talked about schoolwork and the art gallery concert. Raelynn didn't know what Brady had planned for their evening.

They arrived at a local restaurant to begin their evening. It was a small place and was very popular among college students. They both ordered pasta dishes and water. Raelynn loved the breadsticks there. They were the absolute best thing she had ever tasted.

During dinner, they talked about what they planned to do after graduation. Raelynn was glad that they had gotten to know each other pretty well over the last semester. She was pleased that she had kept an open mind as Claire had told her too.

After dinner, they decided to walk around downtown Greeneville. It was a beautiful little town that Raelynn loved so much. Little gift shops and local stores lined the streets. Almost all of the stores were closed, but a few were lit up. They admired the cute trinkets in the window displays. After their walk, they went to Dairy Queen and got ice cream. They took their ice cream and drove down by the lake. They ate their ice cream and watched the sun finish setting.

"Isn't this sunset gorgeous?" Raelynn asked.

"Yes. I am always amazed at how beautiful God's creation is," Brady replied.

After they finished their ice cream, Brady took Raelynn back to her apartment and walked her to the door.

"I had a really nice time tonight," Raelynn said and smiled.

"I did too. Can we do this again sometime?" Brady said.

"I would love that," Raelynn replied.

Raelynn went into her apartment, closed the door behind her, and smiled.

"How was the date?" Claire asked as Raelynn walked in.

"It was really good," Raelynn replied.

"Tell me all about it," Claire said.

"Well, he handed me these flowers, and then we went to that new little restaurant downtown. I forget the name of it. Anyway, it was really good. We both had pasta dishes and breadsticks. Then we walked around downtown and just talked. After that, we got ice cream from Dairy Queen. We went down by the lake and watched the sun set while we ate our ice cream. Then we came back here, and he asked if we could go on another date sometime, and I said yes.

"I am really glad that we had this past semester to get to know each other. It wasn't awkward at all and the date went well. Talking to him is so easy. I'm comfortable around him. I really like him, Claire."

"Raelynn, that's good to hear. I'm happy and excited for you. Plus those flowers are gorgeous."

"Oh, thanks. I really appreciate it. Thank you for being here for me. I cannot tell you how thankful I am that I have such a good friend like you."

Raelynn and Claire talked a little while longer before they headed to bed. Raelynn had to get up early for work the next day. She and Regan had to get some final things done before next week's concert, and Reagan had asked her to come in a little early to help.

Raelynn got ready for bed and put her flowers in

a vase. She brought them into her room and placed them on top of her dresser. She climbed into bed and lay on her back staring up at the ceiling. Raelynn kept replaying the evening in her mind. She was so happy. She felt like she was on cloud nine.

The next morning, Raelynn rushed to get ready for work. She pinned her hair back up and was thankful the curls had held so well overnight. She put on black dress pants and a purple blouse and slid her black flats on. Raelynn did her makeup quickly and then put on a light jacket. She poured coffee into her travel mug, grabbed her keys and purse, and ran to her car. She had never been late for work and would not start now.

If she pulled this concert off, she would get the internship at the art gallery. She really wanted that job. She was practically interning now, but there were a lot of things interns did in addition to being a receptionist and Reagan's assistant. Raelynn surprised herself by making it to work at the time she had told Reagan she would be there.

"Good morning," Raelynn said to those she passed on the way to her desk.

Reagan arrived about ten minutes after Raelynn. She immediately called Raelynn into her office. Raelynn grabbed her pen and notebook and went in.

"Have a seat," Reagan said.

Raelynn sat down. They talked for close to two hours about the concert. They decided that they would set up the stage and the tables on Wednesday to make Thursday easier. On Thursday, they would put the food and drinks out and check the sound. The doors would open at six thirty, and Brady would begin playing at seven o'clock after Reagan introduced him. Reagan and Raelynn decided to leave the two adjacent hallways by the stage open but to block off everything else. Raelynn said she would come to work at five o'clock to help finish setting up. That way, she would have time to run home after class, drop her things off, change, and pick up Claire.

Raelynn walked back to her desk and made some calls to the vendors. She needed to verify that the vendors would arrive at five thirty to set the food up. She and her coworkers had planned to slide the furniture up against the walls so that everything would be out of the way. Raelynn emailed Brady that he needed to be at the gallery at six o'clock for the sound check. She also told him that she would remind him after their school presentation.

At noon, Claire walked through the doors into the gallery. Raelynn didn't even see her because she was focused on getting the last round of ads sent to the newspapers.

"Hey, Raelynn. Working hard I see," Claire said.

Raelynn looked up at her roommate and said, "Hi! What are you doing here?"

"You forgot your lunch, so I decided to drop it off before going to work."

"Oh, thanks. I really appreciate it. I hope you will have a good day today." Raelynn took the brown paper bag from Claire and smiled.

"Well, I've got to get to work. I'll see you back at home. I hope that you will also have a good rest of your day. Bye!" Claire said as she was leaving.

Raelynn called out, "Bye! Thanks again."

The rest went by quickly. By the end of the day, Raelynn had finished getting everything organized for Thursday. She was glad that she had, because that would not only make next week's work easy but also help her focus more on the concert and her class presentation.

Brady and Raelynn had practiced the presentation a couple of times, but Raelynn needed to read through her notecards and view the slides a few more times. She was thankful that she could work on homework when the day was slow at work. She was planning on doing this a few days next week.

By time Raelynn got home and ate dinner, she was exhausted from such a long day. She talked with Claire for a while and then headed to bed. Before falling asleep, Raelynn replied to some text messages from Brady and told him that she would see him Monday.

Chapter 10

The time between Sunday and Tuesday went by faster than Raelynn thought was possible. She was glad that the semester was coming to a close. Next week were finals, and at the end of the week, she would graduate.

Reagan had given her the internship but said that she would have two weeks off before the internship started. Raelynn planned on going to visit her parents after she graduated. She missed them and hadn't seen them since Christmas. She was really looking forward to driving back up to the cottage. She was a little sad that her parents could not make it down for graduation but understood that they did not want to travel so far.

Claire had decided to go with Raelynn. She was really looking forward to seeing the cottage in the woods that Raelynn had always talked about. Claire thought that Raelynn was making some of it up because it sounded way too good to be true.

It was a slow day at work on Wednesday, so they decided to start setting up early. Reagan and Raelynn blocked off some of the hallways in the museum. They set up tables and chairs for the guest to sit at. They set up the table for the appetizers and drinks. Lastly, they put the stage together and blocked the front of it off. They had decided that they would push all the furniture against the walls at five thirty on Thursday night. That way everyone could get in a little overtime.

After everything was set up, Reagan and Raelynn went into Reagan's office. They went over the plan for the next day to make sure that everything would be in order. Raelynn had put a check mark next to everything that was finished. Everything for Wednesday had been checked off. She read Thursday's list to Reagan.

"That sounds good to me. You've done a great job, Raelynn. I am thrilled to have you interning here," Reagan smiled and said.

"I've had a lot of fun planning this event with you. I am looking forward to this opportunity you have given me," Raelynn replied.

"Just so you know, the series of artwork you submitted will go on display May 31st. So when you get back from your two-week break, we'll have to plan that event. We will have a lot to discuss," Reagan said.

"Oh, thank you!" Raelynn said with excitement. "I'm looking forward to that. I'll see you tomorrow at five."

"Have a good night."

"Thank you. You too."

Raelynn gathered her things and headed to her apartment. She was beaming with joy as she walked through the door. She told Claire everything that had happened at work. Claire screamed and hugged her friend. They were both so excited. Brady had been texting throughout the evening and seemed really excited when Raelynn told him about her exhibit and internship.

At school the next day, Brady and Raelynn were the second group out of three that day who gave its presentation. Their presentation went better than they thought that it would. Afterward, their classmates told them that they really enjoyed their presentation and learned a lot. Professor Barker walked up to them after class and congratulated them on how well they presented the Industrial Revolution in art. He asked them where they had gotten the idea, and they told him that they were both artists—he was a musician and she was a painter. Professor Barker seemed very pleased with them. They left the classroom and walked toward the parking lot.

"I really do think we did a great presentation," Brady said.

"I do too. I don't think that our classmates were expecting anything on art. We definitely thought outside of the box," Raelynn replied.

"So what time do I need to be at the gallery tonight?"

"You need to be there by six o'clock. Doors will open at six thirty."

"Okay, I'll be there. Is jeans and a T-shirt okay?"

"As long as it's a nicer looking shirt. Everyone working the event will be dressed up."

"Okay, cool. Do you want to get ice cream after the concert?"

"I would love too. I'll see you tonight."

"Sweet. See you at six."

Raelynn got into her car and headed to her apartment. She did not have much time to change before she had to be at the event.

She got to the apartment, went to her room, and put her bag and books down. She came out and ate dinner with Claire quickly. They both brushed their teeth and changed into black dresses. Claire's boyfriend, Jaden, came over and picked them up. He was dressed in black as well. Raelynn was so glad that they had offered to help work the event. They knew that it was a big deal for Raelynn and wanted to help her out. Raelynn and

Claire grabbed their purses, got into Jaden's car, and headed to the gallery.

Once they got there, they helped clear the entryway by pushing the furniture against the walls, helped set the food and beverages up, and got ready to take tickets and sell ones to those who needed them. Raelynn got out markers so that they would know who had paid and who had not. Everyone had a job and was ready for the event to begin.

Raelynn was surprised how calm everyone was. She was thankful to work with so many amazing people. Reagan was starting to panic because she lost her note cards. Raelynn helped her find her introduction and welcome note cards and had Reagan calmed down within five minutes.

At six o'clock sharp, Brady arrived. He walked in wearing black dress slacks and a black button up shirt. He was carrying his guitar on his back the way he had done the first time she had met him. Raelynn was happy that he had decided to dress up. He looked really nice.

Brady walked over by Raelynn, smiled, and said, "Hi. What should I do?"

Raelynn smiled and replied, "Hi. I have to introduce you to Jeremy. He's running the sound board and will be doing a sound check with you."

Raelynn introduced Brady to Jeremy, and they began running the sound check. Brady went through three songs even though he had a set of seven. He had mostly brought covers but said that he was going to play two originals from his new album, which was soon to be released.

Reagan walked over to Raelynn and told her that she had done a good job and that she was proud of her. That meant a lot to Raelynn, and she was really happy to hear that she had done well.

Raelynn hoped that this evening would go well and fast. She was really looking forward to going out with Brady afterward. It would technically be their second date. She couldn't really describe what she felt for him. Raelynn remembered her talk with Joyelle over

Christmas break and thought that this is what she must have felt. She knew that she loved Brady and knew that God would grow their relationship in only the way that He could.

At six thirty, the doors opened and Reagan had estimated correctly. They had collected almost three hundred tickets and had sold close to two hundred tickets at the door. People from all over Tennessee came. Reagan always had a large crowd when she hosted events.

Everyone gathered around the stage and waited for the show to begin. At seven o'clock, Reagan went up on stage and welcomed everyone. She explained that after the show there were appetizers and beverages available to those who wanted to stick around and visit. She also told them about the hallways that were open to look at art but asked that they would not go past the marked off areas. Then she introduced Brady. The crowd cheered. Raelynn had never remembered seeing a crowd so excited to watch a college student perform, but she hoped that it would go well.

The crowd interacted with Brady. They sang along with his cover songs and stood respectfully when he played his originals. Raelynn stood by Claire and Jaden over by the beverage table. Brady played one original song to start and then five of his most popular cover songs. He finished with an original.

When the show was over, people flocked to the food and drink tables. Reagan told Raelynn and her friends that they didn't need to help clean up and that she would see Raelynn the next day. Raelynn said goodbye and then they walked over by the stage area. Raelynn introduced Brady to Claire and Jaden, and they all chatted for a while. They took pictures together before they decided it was time to leave. Raelynn told Claire that she was going to ride with Brady, and if Claire needed anything, she could text her. Claire said that was okay and that she would see her at home. Claire and Jaden said goodbye, and Brady went to grab his guitar.

Brady walked back to Raelynn, and she said, "You did a great job tonight. You ready to go?"

He replied, "Thank you. Yes, I'm ready. Did you like the last song I played?"

"Yes, that was my favorite one."

"Good because I wrote it for you."

Raelynn smiled at him. She couldn't believe it. No one had ever written a song for her before. As they walked out the door, Brady held Raelynn's hand. This was the kind of love she had been waiting for.

About the Author

I am a twenty-year-old college student originally from Utah but I currently live in the Upper Peninsula of Michigan. I came to faith when I was five and have always tried to live my life for God. I have always loved to write stories and want to pursue a career as an author.